HAUNTED DELAWARE

Delightfully Dreadful
Legends of the First State

CAROLINE WOODS

HAUNTED DELAWARE

Delightfully Dreadful Legends of the First State

CAROLINE WOODS

Buy Books on the Web Publishers

The cover photo is of Fox Lodge at Lesley Manor, courtesy of Elaine and William Class.

ISBN 0-7414-0345-5

Published by:

INFINITY
PUBLISHING.COM

Infinity Publishing.com
519 West Lancaster Avenue
Haverford, PA 19041-1413
Info@buybooksontheweb.com
www.buybooksontheweb.com
Toll-free (877) BUY BOOK
Local Phone (610) 520-2500
Fax (610) 519-0261

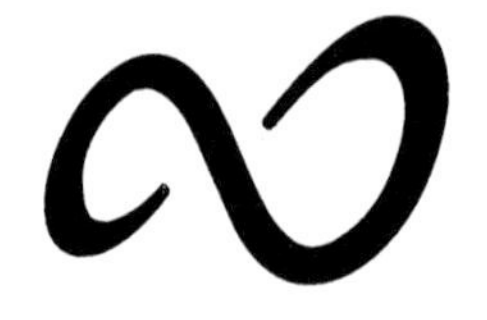

Printed in the United States of America

Printed on Recycled Paper

Published August, 2001

◈ Acknowledgments ◈

I'd like to extend special thanks to the following people for allowing me to interview them:

Joann Perrone
Dolores Michaels
Carolyn Stoebner
Mr. and Mrs. John Clare
Phyllis DeMarco
Elaine Class
Arlene Stockwell
Francine Duncan

I'd also like to thank the following people for their support and encouragement:

Vicki Zwolak
Wendy deCou
Camilla Mancari
Susan Rash
Dave Apostolico

Dedicated to all the ghosts out there:
Thanks for "keepin' it real" . . .

◈ Table of Contents ◈

●In the three marked stories, names have been changed by request. All other names are authentic.

◈ Introduction ◈

Writing this book has been an awesome project that has taken me on a tour of the rich history of Delaware, from wandering the gardens of the Governor's Mansion to peering into actual secret rooms that were built to aid slaves escaping through the Underground Railroad.

It has been a wondrous experience for me. As I did more and more research and interviews, I began to realize how often the fabulously bizarre happens right around us. I began to feel that I had only scratched the surface of what I could find in this state alone. I was dying to know more.

Often while writing these stories I would become so involved in trying to imagine what the characters were feeling that I would scare myself into having to leave the computer and stop writing for a while. Even though it's said that a good book is one that can't be put down, I hope you have the same reaction while reading these stories that I did while writing them.

Caroline Woods
February 2000

WOODBURN
THE SPIRITED GOVERNOR'S MANSION
Dover, Delaware

The stage was set for ghosts to appear.

Cool April breezes were stirring the trees around Woodburn, the Governor's Mansion of Delaware. The moon was full; the air was cold; the warm brick house was aglow in the dark night. An Ouija board had been consulted, and it had stated that the Colonial mansion's famous ghosts were indeed present and ready to show themselves to the current occupants of Woodburn.

The year was 1978, and Pierre S. du Pont IV was the governor of Delaware. He and his wife, Elise, who usually resided in their Rockland, Delaware home, were spending the night in Woodburn in search of the legendary spirits living there. Teamed with two of their children, Benjamin, 14, and Eleuthere, 11, Mrs. du Pont's parents, Mr. and Mrs. Richard Wood, and Mrs. Wood's gray poodle, they all were anxious to do some ghostbusting of their own.

Although they had heard the many stories about the several ghosts inhabiting the house, the spookiest encounter any of them had experienced was Elise du Pont's episodes with a certain portrait of Caesar Rodney. The portrait, which hangs in the dining room, would periodically change position.

But other than that, the family had never seen or heard any of the three (or more) ghosts of Woodburn; therefore, there was a whimsical and slightly skeptical air about the group of ghost-hunters as they settled in for the night.

The governor placed a wine glass full of sherry on the landing of the staircase to entice the "tippling ghost," a spirit of Woodburn who was known to enjoy taking a good drink from some of the previous owners' wine cellars. With that, the du Ponts and the Woods bid one another good night and headed for their separate bedrooms in the three-story brick mansion.

It was then that strange things began to happen. Prior to settling down to sleep, Mrs. Wood left her gray poodle alone in a second-floor bedroom, closing the door behind her. When she returned to the room, the dog was gone. How could a dog have figured his way out of a closed room?

The poodle, wearing a leash and collar with clanging metal tags, was finally found in the basement. Not a soul had heard the dog leave the room, or seen him scurry down the two flights of stairs to the dark cellar.

Meanwhile, three stories above, one of the party opened the door to a third-floor bedroom and found it in complete disarray. The furniture had been overturned and was scattered throughout the room. Resting on the pillow of the bed was a bloodstained handkerchief.

Dismissing the bedroom scene as probably a prank planned by the governor's children, everyone finally went to bed.

All were asleep at two-thirty a.m. when something hit the roof.

The du Ponts in their beds awoke with a start. The house resonated with the sound of large objects hitting and rolling down the roof. It seemed as if someone were dropping dozens of bowling balls from the sky, directly onto the Governor's Mansion.

Governor du Pont, awakened by the crashing sound, sat up in his bed as the noise finally stopped. His eyes widened as he looked out the window. A candle seemed to be floating in the garden, the bobbing light drawing nearer and nearer to the house. Perhaps it was merely because of the dark, but du Pont could see no person holding the candle.

In the midst of the silence, an agonizing female scream ripped through the air. It was coming from outside, and it was very close to the house.

It seemed the entire house was holding its breath. A few seconds passed; then the horrible scream again pierced the night. This time, it was coming from the downstairs hall.

For a moment, nobody moved from his or her bed. Finally, Governor du Pont, in his bare feet and pajamas, decided to get up and see what was going on downstairs. He started out into the corridor and toward the staircase, the others joining him in the wide hallway.

The stairs seemed void of ghosts, but the sleepy-eyed group gasped before anyone set foot on the first step. The wine goblet on the landing was now only one-third full. Not only that, the high-ceilinged front hall was lit not only by the eerie moonlight seeping through the tall windows; a lighted candle had been placed on the second step.

Whatever had been in the garden holding the candle, had it come into the house?

The family wearily went to bed. Stepping into his children's room, the governor checked to make sure they were all right. Scared, the kids asked him to leave their door open and the hall light on. Although he didn't want to frighten them, Governor du Pont did admit, "I think there's something funny going on here."

The light had reappeared in the garden.

On his way back to his room, du Pont glanced at the stairs.

The wineglass was now empty. He hurried down the hall.

Were the strange occurrences at Woodburn that chilly

April night merely an elaborate prank pulled by the du Pont children? Or was the cause of their frightening experience something more unexplainable than that?

Woodburn, built in 1790, is the subject of some of the oldest ghost stories in Delaware. Although the mansion is the perfect picture of beautiful Colonial American architecture, it has been one of the most well-known haunted houses in the state for more than two hundred years. The legends about Woodburn echo throughout Delaware's history, whether exaggerated by firelight from a grandfather to his wide-eyed descendants or whispered by escaping slaves passing through the house on their route north.

With its white pillars, broad windows, warm, wide porches, and facade of pinkish Flemish Bond brick work, Woodburn emits a cheerful, historical feeling. Walking into its grand, high-ceilinged front hall, one can see that the house is a model of exquisite structure and decor, with polished hardwood floors, ornate woodworking, and genuine Colonial furniture, the oldest dating back more than two hundred and fifty years—a very pleasant place to visit, indeed. The possibility of meeting a ghost merely adds to the feeling of enjoyment at seeing such a perfect symbol of American history.

Woodburn was purchased by the State of Delaware to serve as the Governor's House in 1966. Since then, seven of Delaware's governors have lived there. Most of them have come in contact with the more permanent residents of the mansion: the ghosts.

The ghosts have caused many an unusual occurrence in the brick house on Kings Highway. Lights turn on in empty rooms; vases rearrange themselves on shelves; footsteps sound in the large front hall when no one is around.

Who are the unearthly tenants who have been haunting Woodburn for hundreds of years?

This is the (after) life and times of the ghosts of the Governor's Mansion. Woodburn, dubbed "the most haunted house,"[1] not only hosts an unusual number of spooks, it is also home to the most extraordinary assortment of ghostly characters living under one roof.

In the following stories, the italicized segments are fiction, as the author's imagination suggests events in history may have taken place. Everything else is true.

THE GHOST OF CHARLES HILLYARD

A shot rang through the air, followed by a scream from inside the house and the acrid smell of gunpowder. The young man ran as fast as he could through the gardens and around the west wing of his home, panting and out of breath. He slipped for a second on the dewy grass. As he regained his footing, he cocked his head back for a split second and saw his attacker, chasing madly behind him with a deadly gleam in his eye, waving his pistol wildly. The young man turned and continued to run from his father.

Woodburn was built in 1790 by a man named Charles Hillyard, on a piece of land that had been given to his great-

---

[1] Anderson, Jean, "The Most Haunted House," The Haunting of America: Ghost Stories From Our Past (Boston: Houghton Mifflin, 1973.)

grandfather by William Penn. In the fall of 1998, Woodburn began to undergo renovation. One of the primary objects of repair was the magnificent white door on the north porch, which is a double door split in half width-wise. While the workers were restoring the door, stripping off the many layers of paint that had accumulated over the years, they discovered a peculiarly deep hole about six feet from the threshold.

The charred hole was quite obviously not an ordinary knot in the wood. It was a bullet hole.

The son scrambled onto the brick porch steps, tearing one of the knees of his britches in his haste. He could hear the cries of the women inside as his father came screaming after him. "You ingrate! I feed you and clothe you your whole life, and now you think I'll fund your moving to New York to be a low-grade writer! It'll happen over my dead body!"

Charles was gaining on his son, who had opened the front or "main" door to the house and was clambering inside. "Mealy-mouthed coward!" Charles bellowed. In his rage, he quickly aimed and fired his pistol directly at his son's head. At exactly the same time, the son closed the massive front door of the mansion and the bullet sank into the wood.

The finding of the bullet hole, which is now set behind a piece of glass for the visiting public to view, confirmed one of Woodburn's oldest stories.

Charles Hillyard, the man who commissioned the building of the mansion, was a fiery character in life. He is written of as being an "eccentric and tyrannical"[2] man with a hot temper. One story says that he used to amuse himself by making his ten children suffer. He would sit in the great hall and force all of his young ones to stand on their toes for hours, whipping their feet with a riding-crop when they would fall to their heels in exhaustion.

One of the most famous legends about him concerns an argument old Charles had with one of his sons. Judge George Purnell summarized the story quite well when he wrote in 1824:

> " . . . Old Mr. Hillyard in a fit of passion chased his son, pistol in hand, and fired at him just as he went into the north door which was a double door cut in two, horizontally. The son saved his bacon by slamming the door to and the ball entered the door."

At least, that is how the story went. For two hundred years the tale of Woodburn's first owner was told and retold. Many believed it was merely another legend about the allegedly uproarious Mr. Charles Hillyard.

With the discovery of the hole in the door, fiction became fact.

Charles Hillyard passed away in 1814. Following Mr. Hillyard's departure, the house was purchased by his daughter and her husband, Dr. and Mrs. Martin Bates.

Early one particularly gray, overcast morning in

---

[2] Townsend, George Alfred. The Entailed Hat, or Patty Cannon's Times. New York: Harper & Bros., 1883.

1815, Mrs. Bates was in the dining room setting the table for breakfast, with the assistance of a young kitchen maid. She set three place settings, two for herself and her husband, and one for the guest they were entertaining, Lorenzo Dow, the renowned itinerant Methodist preacher.

As steaming hot breakfast was being brought out of the kitchen, Dr. Bates came into the room, followed a few minutes later by Reverend Dow. The minister looked at the three place settings at the table, slightly puzzled, but he did not say a word and his hosts did not notice his perplexity.

The three sat down at the table, but hesitated to raise their forks, waiting for the blessing. There was a momentary pause, and then Mrs. Bates politely asked the good Reverend if he would bless their meal.

"But shouldn't we wait for the other guest before the blessing is offered?" Reverend Dow replied innocently.

After a pause, Mrs. Bates whispered coldly, "There is no other guest in this house."

"But I passed him on the stairs, an older gentleman—"

She answered hastily. "You must be mistaken. We have no other guests."

Puzzled but not willing to start an argument, Lorenzo Dow blessed the meal and they began eating their breakfast in silence.

Before the Reverend left that evening, Mrs. Bates caught him and spoke to him in secret. She asked him who, or what, he had encountered.

He told her he had passed an elderly man on the landing of the stairs between the first and second floor. The man was dressed in old-fashioned knee breeches, a ruffled shirt, and a powdered wig. Dow had nodded a cordial greeting to the old man, and the man had done the same. No words had been exchanged between the two.

Lorenzo Dow had confirmed her fears; the man he described perfectly fit the description of her late father, of whom she and her nine brothers and sisters had always been more than a little afraid. She, too, had caught glimpses of a man in colonial fashions wandering around the house and was beginning to wonder if the ghost of her tyrannical father haunted the house. Mrs. Bates pleaded that the minister not speak to anyone of his encounter with her father's apparition.

Lorenzo Dow was never invited to Woodburn again.

There are no recorded sightings of Charles Hillyard until over fifty years later, in 1870, when Judge George P. Fisher was the owner of Woodburn.

George Fisher, Jr. was home from college for Christmas and had brought a friend to stay with him during the break. The occurrence happened at bedtime during their first night at Woodburn.

The guest was given the room that is known today as the "ghost room": the bedroom that was occupied by the late Charles Hillyard when he was alive. Candles in hand, the two young men went into their separate rooms, bidding each other good night in the hallway.

The door to his room creaked open. A dim glow coming from the blaze in the fireplace illuminated the four-post bed and dresser. That's odd, the young man thought. The fire had obviously been well stoked, yet Mr. and Mrs. Fisher and the servants were fast asleep. It was quite late at night, as he and George had stayed up very late talking and playing cards.

He placed his candlestick on top of the dresser. Out of the corner of his eye something stirred in one of the chairs by the fire. Someone was sitting there!

The young man barely had time to back up as a tall old man in colonial dress slowly stood up from one of the chairs. He was wearing a powdered wig and knee breeches.

His eyes burning into the boy's face, the old man began to walk quickly toward him, jerking his arms and legs in some bizarre charade. George's friend opened his mouth and screamed just before he hit the floor.

George Jr. had barely begun to undress in his own room when he heard a loud scream, then a crashing thud coming from the room where he had left his friend. He ran into the other room and found his friend fainted on the floor. After regaining consciousness, he described the menacing old man who had seemingly tried to force him out. By the time George Jr. had arrived in the room, there was no fire in the fireplace and the old man, presumably the ghost of Charles Hillyard, was gone.

Aside from being a fierce old bat, Charles Hillyard is also described as being one who loved a good drink. Apparently his taste for wine, especially sherry, continues beyond the grave. From time to time, he helps himself to some of the better wines in Woodburn's cellar.

On several occasions Dr. Frank Hall, the last private owner of the mansion, went to his wine cellar and found a bottle mysteriously emptied, but still placed neatly in its rack. The missing wine was usually the best or most rare vintage in the house. Woodburn is proud to host the only known ghostly wine connoisseur in the state.

The late Governor Charles L. Terry, Jr. enjoyed the presence of the "tippling ghost," or "wino." He was known to tell amusing stories about the ghost, saying that many of the previous owners of the house would leave decanters full of wine out before they went to bed, and without fail, the decanters would be empty in the morning.

Governor Terry himself often left glasses of wine out for the ghost, which would slowly be drained. He never actually saw the ghost drinking the wine, but every time someone would walk by, a little more of the wine would be gone until the glass was empty.

One of Governor Terry's servants swears that he actually did see the ghost of Charles Hillyard once, having a drink of wine. Glancing into the dining room as he walked by, the servant saw an old man in colonial dress, seated at the table. He was slowly drinking red wine from a decanter. When the servant did a double take and went back to look at the apparition, the elderly man was gone. All that was on the table was the half-filled decanter.

The ghost of Charles Hillyard is more often heard

than seen. As often as once a week, footsteps can be heard pacing in the great front hall or walking up and down the stairs from the first floor to the second floor. Almost all of the people employed at the Governor's Mansion have heard the heavy pacing in the main hall when they are alone in the house, only to peek in and find that there is no one there. At least, they find no living souls.

Security guards often stay alone at Woodburn until very late at night, keeping watch over the Governor's Mansion. Often when a guard is deep into a game of solitaire in the dining room, he or she will hear what sounds like someone pacing on the hardwood floor in the front hall. The guard goes into the hall to investigate and finds no one there. After a brief search of the entire downstairs, the security guard returns to the dining room.

The cards have been recklessly scattered all over the table.

Charles Hillyard causing trouble?

In late 1998 a woman was hired to stencil the small bathroom under Woodburn's staircase. As she was painting the walls of the restroom with curling green ivy, she kept hearing loud footsteps on the wooden stairs above her. Even though she knew she was alone in the house, it sounded as if a man were walking up and down the stairs. She would come out of the bathroom repeatedly, paintbrush in hand, but she never saw who was making the noise.

The woman had never heard Woodburn's legends before, but when she told the docents who operate the tours in the Governor's Mansion, they were not surprised. They told her it was merely the specter of the late Charles Hillyard, constantly watching over the beautiful home he built two hundred years ago.

LITTLE GIRL IN A RED DRESS

The sweetest of all the Woodburn ghosts is a little girl wearing a red gingham dress and bonnet. She has appeared standing at the reflecting pool behind the gardens. She carries a lit candle and does not seem menacing or spectral; rather, she is preoccupied, as small children often are, playing by the bank of the pool.

The reflecting pool, which sits among the formal gardens of Woodburn, was added between the years 1912 and 1918, while Senator Daniel Hastings owned the house. Therefore, the little girl is Woodburn's "newest" ghost, first appearing during the twentieth century.

Although it has been more than fifty years since the mysterious little girl has actually been seen, she has been encountered in a different fashion on several occasions.

The year was 1985, and Mike Castle had just been elected Governor of the State of Delaware. Woodburn was hosting an inaugural ball held in his honor. All present were having a marvelous time.

However, amidst the sounds of laughter and political conversation in the great house, something else could be heard.

"Ouch!" "Oh!" Someone was tugging on the women's skirts.

Many of the female guests would feel a slight pulling on the hems of their dresses, as if a small hand was trying to get their attention from very low to the ground. The women would whirl around, fully expecting to see a little girl with a mischievous grin smiling up at them.

They would be startled to see nothing at all behind them. Looking around, they would hear a tiny giggle and know that the little tot was running away, dodging the grown-up legs to find her next long-skirted victim.

THE HANGING TREE

It was a neighborhood legend. Hollow and gnarled, with thick, twisting branches writhing upward like human arms, "the hanging tree" would beckon young children who were unfortunate enough to pass by it in the dark. One glance at its massive trunk and the moaning would begin, seemingly coming from deep inside the tree. On Halloween, it would be the loudest.

While filling their sacks with candy, the children would walk as quickly as they could by the tree in Woodburn's yard, whispering so that the ghost wouldn't hear them.

"I hear that tree's a hundred years old!"

"No, no, you got it all wrong. It's gotta be two hundred!"

The infamous tulip poplar lived to be over three hundred and ten years old, as a matter of fact. It was planted in the year 1680. Delaware was a colony of Britain, and it would be two years before William Penn would inherit the "three lower counties of Delaware." The tree was born decades before our founding fathers were. It planted its tiny roots only about sixty years after the landing of the Mayflower on Plymouth Rock.

Unfortunately, the enormous, hollow tree stood too close to Woodburn for comfort, and it had to be taken down in 1997. But even in its absence the tree called "the hanging tree" is still the center of one of Woodburn's greatest stories.

It begins during the antebellum era of the United States, with the great divides between slavery and abolition, union and secession, almost at their bloody pinnacle. Woodburn, having just turned fifty years old, had passed through the hands of several owners. At that time, the Cowgill family, who occupied the house for nearly a hundred years, owned Woodburn. Hence its name from 1825 to 1912: Cowgill House.

The original Cowgill owner was quite an unusual man for his time. Delaware, though it sided with the Union in the Civil War, kept slavery legal until 1863. Especially in Kent and Sussex Counties, many Delawareans continued to hold slaves. Although Mr. Cowgill lived in southern Delaware, he never kept any bondspeople. As a matter of fact, the man was known for treating black people with the same kindness and respect that he gave white folks. Often he was away from home for long periods of time, and it was apparent that during these times he welcomed free black friends to stay in his Dover mansion, which was unheard of in that era.

A peculiar piece that fits into that puzzle is the layout of Woodburn's basement. Unusually enough, one of the walls in the cellar holds a door which, when opened, leads to nothing but the cold brown earth of the outside ground.

The door once led to a secret tunnel. Traveling underneath Woodburn's grounds, the underground passage led directly to the St. Jones River. Often, in the middle of the night, shadowy figures would come out of the tunnel, darting into rowboats marked with a yellow light above a blue one . . . and what of the fact that old Mr. Cowgill happened to be a Quaker? Yes, Woodburn, called Cowgill House at the time, was once part of the legendary Underground Railroad.

Because of its connections with the Railroad and the number of African-Americans frequently in the home during the Cowgill ownership, Woodburn was a major target for slave kidnappers. These outlaws captured free black people and escaped slaves and sold them south for a high price. Legend has it that the infamous and terror-inspiring Ms. Patty Cannon herself led a raid on Woodburn.

Standing over six feet tall, holding a horse whip in her brawny, mannish hand, the notorious kidnapper and murderess made the people of Delaware, black and white, tremble with fear. There is proof that she brutally slaughtered over forty people in her lifetime before she committed suicide in a Delaware prison the night before her scheduled hanging.

It may have been during this mistress of death's raid on the mansion one frigid October night that the soul of a man became trapped on Woodburn's grounds forever.

Patty's band of cutthroats surrounded the house and swarmed inside, bursting down doors and crashing through windows, armed with bludgeons, knives, and whips, sending all those inside running in terror.

The tree!

Its enormous trunk with its deep, hollow center glowed like a beacon of hope in the gloomy night. Amidst the chaos in the house behind him, Tommy began to trot quickly toward the old tulip poplar tree.

Before he could turn around to see if anyone was watching him, a rusty chain fell around his neck and was yanked back, causing him to gasp and choke.

"I got one! Ha! Ha! Caught myself a big, strong buck!" Pale white arms were around Tommy's broad shoulders as he struggled to release himself from the man's grasp.

"Hey, what you doin', boy? You comin' with me!" He yanked the chain tighter around Tommy's neck, cutting off more of his air.

As the white man started to drag his gasping captive back to the house, ranting about how he was "bringin' ole Patty one of 'em uppity free Negroes," Tommy thought back to the one glimpse he had caught of "ole Patty". She had looked him directly in the eye the second after she kicked in the back door with one enormous leg, and it had been a look of such utter evil and malice that it made him nauseated to think of her. He had to get away from his captor, and he had to do it quickly.

In a desperate motion, Tommy swung his right leg around as hard as he could, kicking the other man in the back of his knees and causing both of them to stumble to the ground. Tommy scrambled to his feet. The white man let out a growl of surprise and reached inside his thin black jacket, fumbling for a knife before Tommy kicked him square in the ribs. Howling with pain, the man curled up on the ground and his prisoner, now free from his grasp, turned and ran for the ancient tree.

The hole in the trunk looked barely wide enough for Tommy's shoulders to squeeze through, and he hesitated. His plan was to hide in the hollow of the tree until the kidnappers were gone. Dark and moist inside, the tree's deep middle seemed almost as frightening as the prospect of being sold into slavery. But the picture of Patty Cannon's frigid gray eyes flashed into his mind, and Tommy dove headfirst into the empty trunk.

As he slipped inside he realized that the cavity in the tree was actually much narrower than he had expected. His legs slid fully into the trunk and tried to find their footing and push him upright, but there simply was not enough room. Tommy was stuck upside down in a space not much bigger than he.

Tommy began to panic, as the slimy walls of the inside of the ancient plant seemed to close in on him. He desperately clawed with hands and feet to right himself as he felt the tiny legs of the insect inhabitants of the rotting inner trunk crawling over his sickened face and up toward his neck. His large, powerful fists beat as hard as they could on the inside of the tree as Tommy yowled and screamed, rattling the chain still looped around his neck, the tormented sounds reaching not one of the panicked ears inside the house.

The blood-freezing moans and the rattling of chains, which drifted in and out of the massive tulip poplar tree, were always stronger when the moon was bright and full, particularly on Halloween.

Legend says that the appalling shrieks, which sounded for decades from inside the gnarled, twisted trunk, were those of a black man escaping from a band of kidnappers raiding Woodburn. Hiding from his captors in the tree's deep trunk, the man became trapped in the narrow recesses of the tulip poplar, never to see sunlight again.

When the centuries-old Hanging Tree was cut down, the moans of one of the famed ghosts of Woodburn fell along with it. The ghost was finally freed from his botanical tomb.

As life replaces life, a new, young tulip poplar, planted by Governor Mike Castle in 1987 (by tradition, each Delaware governor plants a tree at Woodburn), now stands very close to the place once occupied by the legendary Hanging Tree.

Planted in that hallowed spot, what fate awaits this youthful tree?

THE GRANDFATHER CLOCK

Wilmington, Delaware

Grace opened her eyes. The clock by her bed read 2 A.M. Ever since her husband had passed away a month before, she hadn't been getting much sleep. This particular night was not one of the better ones. The sixty-three-year-old Wilmington resident rolled over again and tried to find a more comfortable position. She had slept fitfully all night and would awaken with a deep longing to have her husband, Don, beside her.

Grace, a former teacher, had been alone in her stately Rockford Tower-area home since Don's heart attack had hospitalized him two months before. A second heart attack had proved fatal and had sent her into deep mourning for her lost husband. Her children had been urging her to sell the house, and Grace was reluctantly beginning to succumb to their urgings. As much as she loved her home, she had to admit that it was a lot of work to maintain and it was too cold and lonely without her husband.

Finally, after much tossing and turning, Grace decided to go downstairs and read for a while. She glanced at the digital clock before she left the bedroom. It was 2:38.

Grace made her way downstairs. “I went to the bookshelves in the den. Suddenly I felt a terrible longing to be able to see Don. I was overcome with a feeling of grief, so strong that I had to sit down.” Grace collapsed wearily into a soft, plush chair by the fireplace.

Just then there was a knock at the front door.

It started as a low tap. Then the sound grew louder and louder, until it became a steady rapping on the large front door. Grace forgot her grieving for a second. “I was scared to death. I was thinking to myself, who would be coming to see me at this hour? It could be an intruder or someone bearing bad news. Either way, I was scared of what was behind that door. I could see the door from where I was sitting, but I couldn't move.”

Grace shakily rose to her feet. At once the pounding stopped. Confronting her fears, she went to the door and peeked through the peephole.

There was no one there. Thinking that maybe she had not been able to see the caller through the darkness, she slowly opened the door. No one.

At this point, Grace was getting curious, yet still very scared. She peered to the sides of the porch and out onto the street, staying inside the doorframe for protection. She could see no one. The street was hushed and still, laced with the shadows of tree branches.

Even though there was no one in sight, Grace could feel that there was someone there with her. "It wasn't a threatening presence, but it did make me feel uncomfortable. I had never felt anything like that before. It was an uneasy feeling. There was an eerie silence. No wind blew. No dogs barked. Nothing made a sound." Grace was about to close the door in a hurry when something broke the silence.

A faint *whirr* came from the next room, followed by the chimes of a grandfather clock declaring the time, 2:45 A.M.

Don's uncle had given the two of them a beautiful mahogany grandfather clock as a wedding present forty years before. A family heirloom, the clock had been specially ordered from Germany for his uncle's first wife, who had passed away at the young age of thirty-one. Don had always cherished the clock, taking great pride in the fact that his uncle chose to give the clock to him instead of Don's older sister. He had taken care to make sure to wind the clock regularly, so that the sound of Westminster chimes always filled the warm brick house.

Ever since Don's death, Grace had put the clock out of her mind with all of her grief. No one had wound the clock since the last day he had been home, over two months ago. Since then the clock had stood silent at its post in the large living room near the front of the house. Until that night.

"I didn't even realize what was happening, at first. I almost jumped out of my slippers when I heard the chimes, but it took me a few seconds to realize that the clock had not been wound in over two months. Don had been the only one who had ever wound the clock, and he was gone."

Grace turned and went into the living room. The towering clock looked unearthly in the shadowy room, pendulum swinging, keeping perfect time.

As soon as Grace saw that the clock was running, she lost all fear. "I knew that Don had come back and wound the clock, that he had known how sad I was feeling and that he had come to tell me that he was all right. I knew then that he would always be with me." Grace's eyes shine with the memory. "I said aloud, 'Thank you, sweetheart. Thank you for visiting me.' Then I wiped away the tears that were running down my face, and went to bed."

Feeling very peaceful and calm, wearing a bittersweet smile, Grace fell asleep with no trouble.

When she awoke the next morning, the clock was silent and still once more. But Grace did not have any doubts about whether the experience of the night before was real. She called her son, Brian, and told him what had happened. He came over and the two of them wound the clock.

Grace has continued to wind the clock regularly, ever since her husband paid her a late night visit. "The clock now keeps me company. I have no doubt that Donald came back to tell me that he loves me, and used the clock to do so. I don't think that he paid me a visit to make sure I would take care of his grandfather clock." She laughs. "Although I do pay more attention to it than I did before!"

THE RED COAT

New Castle, Delaware

A dedicated legal secretary, Phyllis was considered one of the best at the large Wilmington firm where she worked during the day. At night she would hurry home to care for her elderly mother, who lived with her in an apartment in New Castle. Phyllis was hardly the type of person one would expect to be addicted to playing with an Ouija board.

Yet what started out to be a mere few hours of fun became a nightly excursion for Phyllis and her sister. The dial would spell things that the two women hadn't told anyone – not even each other. Though they never truly believed that they were contacting the dead, it was fun making each other a little scared.

The DeMarco sisters had been playing with the Ouija board nightly for a few weeks when the game began to turn morbid and strange. Phyllis could sense something wicked and malicious, as if they had contacted an evil entity. When during one session the Ouija dial began to spell over and over again the name of Phyllis's youngest daughter, who had died as an infant, she and her sister sprang from their chairs, terrified. The board was banished to the back bedroom.

The Ouija board stayed peacefully stored, and all had been quiet for about a week when Phyllis's sister brought home a present for their mother. It was a new red jacket. When the jacket turned out to be too small for their mother, Phyllis and her sister decided that it would be nice to give it to the woman who lived in the apartment across the hall. She was about the same age as their mother, but was probably small enough to wear the red coat.

A few days later, Phyllis was coming home from work. She reached the door of her apartment at about the same time the couple from across the hall were walking in their door. Thinking that it would be a good time to give her neighbor the red jacket, Phyllis told her that she would visit in a few minutes. She headed into the back bedroom, where her mother had put the jacket. There it lay, on top of the desk in the corner.

As Phyllis grabbed the coat from the desk, out of the corner of her eye she saw something on the desktop move. There was the open Ouija board. Had the dial just jumped? Phyllis's hands hesitated for a second, then without thinking she placed them on the dial.

Instantly the little game piece began to fly! At first she did not understand what it was spelling, but the message soon became clear, spelling out the same thing, firmly and frantically over and over again:

G. E. T . . . R. I. D . . . O. F . . . T. H. E . . . R. E. D . . . J. A. C. K. E. T . . .

Phyllis's eyes grew wider and wider as her hands darted across the board, guided by the little dial. Finally she pulled them away and her gaze shifted in horror to the red jacket draped across her arm. Should I warn her about the . . . No, she thought. If I start believing what this thing says, then I really will have crossed the line!

She felt sick looking at the again quiet Ouija board on the desk as she left the room. Phyllis gave an incredulous description of what had just happened to her mother and sister. They of course thought that the notion of a simple coat being dangerous was crazy, and Phyllis agreed. She walked out her door and across the hallway to present the coat to her neighbor.

The day after receiving the generous gift of a new coat from her friends, the woman across the hall suffered a tragic stroke. She stayed in the hospital for nearly three months, never regaining the strength she needed to live. For the rest of her days, the lady was confined to a wheelchair.

Yet she never learned the tale of what had happened the day before disaster struck. The guilt ate away at Phyllis and her mother and sister for not telling their friend the ominous message about the red coat, but still they never spoke a word of it to anyone.

The Ouija board was put away for good: in the trashcan. And the lady across the hall died in the summer of 1999. The red jacket was still hanging in her closet.

AUNT BILLIE

Wilmington, Delaware

When Timmy Eskridge, a twenty-eight year old bachelor, was given the opportunity to buy his great-uncle's and -aunt's house after they passed away, he thought it would be the perfect home for a single guy. What he didn't know was that his deceased Aunt Billie may have never moved out.

The house at 709 Highland Avenue was Billie and Joe Santillo's only home during their sixty years of marriage. After they were married, Joe had quickly gone to work building the young couple's dream house. The two-story stucco dwelling delighted the eager newlyweds.

The two of them filled their home with love and laughter over the next half century. Though they never had any children of their own, Joe and Billie doted on their many nieces and nephews. Though "Aunt Billie" was always very caring and kind to her husband's side of the family, she tended to favor her own nieces and nephews over his. If this bothered Joe he didn't let it show, for he was a gentle man and he loved his wife from the bottom of his heart. Billie was always described as being a "sweet lady, a very kind person."

As the time passed and Billie Santillo grew old, she gradually became incapable of caring for herself. “In sickness and in health,” Joe was always at his wife’s side, even as his own health began to deteriorate. Aunt Billie slipped farther into oblivion, becoming almost completely incoherent. Ironically it was Joe's niece, Joann Perrone, who lived across the street from them, who stepped in to help her elderly uncle care for his wife. Joann would feed her, bathe her, and change her as if she were caring for a newborn child, even though Aunt Billie could not even remember who Joann was.

In early 1998, Billie had been completely bedridden for four years when Joe was diagnosed with a brain tumor and was rushed to the hospital. Aunt Billie was placed in the care of a nursing home.

Late at night on January 5, 1998, the night of Uncle Joe’s surgery for his brain tumor, the hospital called Joann at home to tell her that he had just taken a turn for the worse. The nurse told Joann that her uncle was not expected to live through the night.

Less than half an hour later, another of Aunt Billie’s nieces received a similar phone call. Aunt Billie had been taken from the nursing home to the hospital because of congestive heart failure. The doctors there predicted that she, too, would never again see daylight.

Both of them survived the night. Maybe it was their extreme closeness that caused their health to plunge at the same time, and the strength of mutual love that kept them both alive.

Yet Billie’s health continued to rapidly deteriorate, and she died one cold February day in 1998. Her husband, Joe, never regained his strength. Alone without Billie, he passed away on October 13, 1998.

A month after Uncle Joe died, Timmy Eskridge, a great-nephew on Uncle Joe's side of the family, purchased the Santillo house from the estate. Prior to November 1998 Timmy was a staunch unbeliever in ghosts. But immediately after he moved in, Timmy noticed some very strange things happening in the old house.

Indistinct, muffled moans echoed through the walls in a chillingly sad, obviously female voice. The kitchen chairs moved right before Timmy's astonished eyes. Joann reported that from her house across the street she frequently saw the kitchen lights go on by themselves when he was not at home. Indeed, most of the peculiar happenings in the house occur in the kitchen, which was Aunt Billie's favorite room when she was alive.

Timmy would often feel a noticeable chill when he awoke in the morning, only to check the thermostat to find that the setting had been lowered during the night. Frustrated, Timmy hired an electrician to check the heater. The electrician told Timmy that the heater was working fine. Not sure what he was dealing with, Timmy asked his older relatives, who told him that Billie Santillo liked to lower the heat in the house when she went to sleep. In life she always liked it cold; indeed, his house has a distinct chill which seems to never go away.

Though the thought of his dead Aunt Billie playing with his thermostat and moving his furniture was creepy, Timmy could have dealt with her harmless actions had she not begun to turn violent.

One night, Timmy had just gotten into bed when suddenly the ceramic portable heater sitting on his bureau was heaved across the room by an unseen force, crashing into the floor. Unharmed but very shaken, Timmy left the house and would not return until daylight. After that incident, Timmy became concerned for his young son's safety and no longer let the boy spend the night when he visited.

There would be many nights when Timmy would be too scared to go to sleep in the house, afraid of what could happen to him. After spending only one night in Timmy's house, his girlfriend refused to sleep there ever again. The harrowing voice of the dead woman has driven away many of Timmy's friends as well. And his Aunt Joann's Boston

Terrier, Mason, won't even cross the street to go anywhere near the house where old Uncle Joe used to give him treats all the time.

Joann began to worry for her nephew's safety. "When I wake up and see that his truck is still there [because he hasn't left for work yet,] I worry that she did something to him during the night." Concerned for Timmy and piqued with a little curiosity, Joann asked her doubting husband, Paul, to spend a night in her uncle's old house. Paul, a complete skeptic about the existence of ghosts, readily accepted the challenge. Very soon after Joann and Paul climbed into bed, they heard sad cries in a woman's voice. Though the sounds were indistinct and low at first, they soon grew louder and more persistent, crying out one word over and over. Joann and Paul could not believe their ears. To Paul it sounded like the voice was screaming, "Joe! Joe!"; Joann thought she heard her saying, "Go! Go!" Was Aunt Billie trying to find Joe, or was she unhappy that her late husband's relatives were occupying the house? Joann and Paul didn't wait to find out. They obeyed the command that Joann heard.

Billie Santillo had always been afraid of death. Truly she did manage to fight the Grim Reaper over many years of illness. But as happens to all of us, time caught up with her in the end. Perhaps it is her fear of the unknown that has made her cling to the home she enjoyed so much in life, and her confusion in the absence of her beloved Joe that causes her moans to reverberate through her house.

FOX LODGE AT LESLEY MANOR: THE CASTLE

New Castle, Delaware

Fox Lodge at Lesley Manor in historic New Castle looks the part of the ultimate haunted house. Walking up the path to the creamy yellow Gothic Revival mansion, crowned with maroon gingerbread trim and shaded by towering trees with long-hanging branches, one gets the feeling of visiting an enchanting country inn in a Gothic Victor Hugo novel. Gargoyles glare, mouths gaping, perched on ivy-covered stone walls. Light streams through stained glass windows. The house remains in the shadow of the great trees, even in broad daylight, except for the tower. The most prominent feature of the house—for that matter, the entire area—is the imposing tower jutting out of the landscape, announcing the presence of the grand mansion which appears to be from another time.

The mansion seems the perfect place to find centuries-old spirits walking the grounds . . . hidden rooms and secret passageways . . . invisible figures stirring on staircases . . . voices that drift in from nowhere. . . antiquated skeletons wrapped in chains. . .

Lesley Manor hosts all of the aforementioned curiosities and more.

The mansion itself, built in 1855, and its original owners, Dr. Allan Vorhees Lesley and his wife, Jane, are encircled in mystery. Legends of the house and its mysterious owners have surfaced time and again. Some have proved true; some have been left unsolved for the curious to ponder.

Elaine and William Class bought Lesley Manor, which is listed on the National Register of Historic Buildings, in 1994. As well as making the Victorian mansion their residence, the Classes opened Fox Lodge, a bed and breakfast, in the house. It didn't take long for the spirits to present themselves to their new tenants.

The presence of ghosts in the mansion adds to its charming mystique. "I have never felt threatened for one moment in the house," says Elaine Class with a warm smile. Indeed, there is a sense of comfort about Lesley Manor, as if gentle spirits are watching over those who visit their home.

The following is a collection of the legends and corresponding truths about Delaware's most incredible mansion. The pieces in italics are historical fiction, inspired by legend. Everything else is pure fact.

"What that noise, Papa?"

Jacob froze at the sound of crackling in the night. His daughter's hands tightened around his neck as he looked sharply to his left, wide-eyed and afraid. Elisa knew to be absolutely silent so that he could listen to see who was there.

For two weeks the two of them had been traveling through the dense Delaware forests, hiding during the day, running through the thick brush in the night, crossing deep streams to avoid being chased by dogs. Since they had escaped from their former master's farm in Maryland, the conductors of the Underground Railroad had been their main source of food, shelter, and refuge from the pursuit of the oppressor, who they felt was always breathing down their necks.

Branches crackled again, closer to their feet. Peering into the brush, Jacob spied the fleeting tail of a gray squirrel darting up a tree. He let out the breath he had been holding in. "Ain' nothin', baby."

Elisa loosened her grip on his neck. Jacob continued to walk quickly toward the northeast. He followed both the North Star and the compass given to him by the Quaker man living at the last house where the pair had sought refuge. The kind man had taken a shine to the little girl's big, beautiful eyes.

The harsh trip north had been hard on the girl, who was only eight years old. She could not match her father's quick strides that were necessary to cover ample ground in the black of night. Lack of sleep and little food had given her once plump cheeks a sunken look. Her already weary father had to carry her for much of the way, yet not for a minute did he regret taking his child with him to freedom.

The plantation owner's selling of Elisa's mother into the Deep South six months before had driven Jacob and his daughter to plan an escape. When word spread that the master was thinking of selling Jacob also, which would have forced him to leave Elisa forever, he had decided to take the dangerous route north to Philadelphia.

Jacob caught a glimpse of purplish light beginning to

seep through the trees. Dawn was coming. They had to find the next house before sunrise or search the woods for cover and risk being seen.

He took his daughter's small hand in his large, rough one. "Jes' a bit longer, child, 'til we rest."

Soon after Elaine Class purchased Lesley Manor, she realized that there is quite literally more to the house than meets the eye.

Rumors circulated about hidden rooms and passageways inside the mansion. These were confirmed when Elaine inherited the original building plans for the house. Although the secret rooms were not on the blueprint, the contractor had written on the plans that he had built two hidden chambers in the house. However, to ensure absolute secrecy, he did not include the location of these rooms. Mr. and Mrs. Class were left to find secret places that not a living soul had seen in nearly a century.

No one had any idea where they were.

The house Jacob and his daughter gazed upon was nothing like his former master's white plantation house in Maryland. Working as a coachman, Jacob had seen quite a few of the rich planters' homes of southeastern Maryland, but this house was nothing like anything he had ever laid eyes on. It loomed large and yellow in the dusky light. The thick Gothic arches and pointy tower had seemed to appear out of nowhere in the middle of the Delaware forest.

A stone gargoyle silently screamed at the pair. "This the house?" Jacob thought to himself. He was about to turn back when the large front door opened and a dignified man in a robe set one foot out of the door, peering at Jacob. Elisa stood close by him, hugging his legs.

The man beckoned to them with his hand. "Come in, come in! You must be tired," he whispered out into the yard. "We've been expecting you. Come along!"

The inside of the house was dark and extremely large. Drippy candles lit the rooms, causing shadows to play on the staircase and thick woodworking. Without a word, the man led Jacob and Elisa into the towering foyer. They followed him up the steep, wallpapered stairs to the second floor. They had a glimpse of long, dark hallways with tall black doors lit by candle sconces before they followed the man up the staircase to the third floor.

The first hidden room was relatively easy for the Classes to find. While in one of the second-floor bedrooms, they noticed that the ceiling of the room's built-in closet was much lower than the ceiling of the bedroom itself.

The third-floor dining room is directly above that particular second-floor bedroom. Upon going to the corresponding corner in the floor of that dining room, the Classes discovered, to their excitement, a carefully hidden trap door in the hardwood floor.

Under the door they found a brick-lined room, large enough for four people to stand in.

Jacob watched wearily as the man, who had introduced himself as Allan Lesley, pulled up the floorboards in the corner of the room with a screwdriver. Clutching his daughter's hand, Jacob could barely keep standing. With the strain on his body, constantly running from almost certain death, the agony of knowing he would never see his wife again, and the uncertainty of whether he and his beautiful girl would ever reach freedom, Jacob was on the verge of collapse. He barely noticed when a pretty, dark-haired woman in a white robe gently pushed a plate of biscuits into his hand.

"Oh, thank you, ma'am!" Jacob could barely contain his hunger. He knelt and offered some of the food to his daughter, who grabbed a biscuit hungrily.

"Later I'll have the cook make you both a hot meal. This will tide you over until then." She smiled kindly at Jacob.

By then, Dr. Lesley had pulled up the remaining floorboards, revealing a large square hole in the floor. "It's quite cramped in there, but of course you don't need to hide unless someone should come looking for you. Get some sleep. You need it. We'll wake you later to have a good lunch."

"Thanks so much, sir, ma'am."

The doctor nodded, then he and his wife left the room quietly.

Yellow light was now starting to peek around the sides of the heavy curtains. Two small beds were set up in the corner, with fluffy blankets and pillows. Jacob led his little one over to one of the cots. Elisa let out a small sigh and sank her head into the deep pillow, curling up under the soft covers. Jacob sat beside her on the small bed, massaging her little back with a hand that was almost as wide as her shoulders. When her breathing grew heavy, he knew she had fallen asleep. For such a young girl to be so sleep-starved for so long was not very healthy, Jacob knew. He only hoped the joy of being free would be worth the harrowing journey.

He and his daughter had never known what it was like to wake up in the morning and think, "I am my own person. Where will life lead me today?" Jacob thought of his grandmother, who had been viciously torn from her family in Africa, his wife, who was somewhere far away, still toiling for another man's benefit, and his daughter, who had been "licked by the strap" often enough to make Jacob's heart ache with anger.

Tears came to his eyes. Yes, it would be worth the grueling quest north to have even a taste of independence. No matter how hard the journey, Jacob would gain the freedom Elisa deserved.

The second hidden room was much harder to find. Mrs. Class found it while she was in the process of turning the former butler's pantry, which is really quite large, into her kitchen.

While reforming the old dumbwaiter into a pantry, she and her daughter discovered that the "ceiling" of the dumbwaiter was not a ceiling at all. It was merely a piece of wood that could be moved easily. Upon sliding out the piece of wood, Elaine discovered a large amount of space directly above the butler's pantry's ceiling, almost thirty inches tall and covering about twelve square feet—big enough for someone to hide in.

Aside from the two secret rooms, the house's basement hosts an unusual commodity. One door in a certain wall of the basement leads to a tunnel, now collapsed, which ends in the street.

Why on earth would the Lesleys have needed two secret rooms and a secret passageway leading from the basement?

The area where the basement tunnel leads, what is now 7th street in New Castle, was a rather large pond in Dr. Lesley's day. The Lesleys used to own a rowboat, which was conveniently located at the exact spot on the shore of the pond where the tunnel ended.

The theory about Lesley Manor's secret rooms is that the manor used to be a station on the Underground Railroad. Escaped slaves would row across the pond in the middle of the night, travel through the tunnel, climb up the dumbwaiter, and hide in either the room above the butler's pantry or the room below the dining room floor.

There are no records stating any connection the house had to the Underground Railroad, as there rarely are. Letters written by Dr. Lesley have been found, implying that his brother was a Northern enthusiast. Dr. Lesley at some points in his letters seems to agree with the South, but perhaps he was trying to throw off possible slave kidnappers like Ms. Patty Cannon. It seems no one will ever know the truth of Dr. Lesley's involvement with the Underground Railroad, and it merely adds to the enigma that is Allan Vorhees Lesley.

One evening Elaine and her daughter, Lesa Class-Savage, were walking down the back staircase, which leads to the former servants' quarters. Peering into the window at the foot of the stairs was a woman. Her chin was resting on her hands, and she was clearly smiling at the two women through the glass. Suddenly she vanished.

Elaine and Lesa stared at each other. Not quite sure if what they saw was real, they questioned each other as to what they had seen. Their descriptions of the smiling woman matched perfectly.

Was the woman Jane Lesley?

The man who sits in the second floor sitting room has also surprised both women. Elaine has walked in several times to discover an elderly man sitting thoughtfully in the chair by the fireplace, dressed entirely in old-fashioned white clothes. It wasn't until she had encountered him several times that she questioned Lesa about him. Elaine's daughter's description of the man matched her own: a man in white sitting with his legs crossed, his hands on his knees. Directly after one of the sightings, Elaine made a sketch of the man she had seen.

Several months later, the Classes were viewing a slide show that contained pictures of previous owners of Lesley Manor. When a slide of Dr. Allan Lesley, the builder of the house, came onto the screen, Lesa and Elaine gasped.

He looked exactly like the man in Elaine's sketch.

She had matched his hairstyle to a tee. The man in the slide looked several years younger than the man in her drawing, but was clearly the same person the two had encountered sitting by the fireplace.

After doing some more research, Elaine discovered that the room in which the man had been repeatedly spotted was in fact the room where Dr. Allan Lesley treated his patients, hence the all-white clothing of the ghost of the doctor. The room had been a later addition onto the mansion, built several years after the house was finished.

This made sense, since the ghost of Dr. Lesley looked older than the picture, which was taken at about the time the house was built. The room had been a newer addition and the ghost an older apparition.

Lesa and Elaine are not the only ones who have seen the ghosts in their home. In the summer of 1998, Elaine went to her native Ohio and brought back her mother, Millie Pataky, her sister-in-law, and her two young nieces.

Although Elaine's sister-in-law had desperately wanted to meet one of the ghosts, it was Millie, who had previously encountered one of the spirits of Lesley Manor, who again encountered one.

She was spending the night in "Jane's Room," one of the rooms open for rent in Fox Lodge. The room was given the name because it was believed by Elaine and Lesa to be the master bedroom in the original plan of the house.

In the middle of the night, Millie was abruptly awakened. Peering in the dim light coming through the blinds in her room, she saw a woman sitting on the foot of her bed.

The woman, clothed in a flowing white nightgown, was fairly young. With a peaceful look on her face, she stared at Millie for a few seconds. It seemed that she had been there for some time, quietly watching the older woman sleep. Almost directly after Millie had opened her eyes, the apparition vanished into thin air. Jane had come to see who was sleeping in her bedroom.

§

The man and woman make an odd picture, bathed in the blue moonlight of the forest, shackled together at the hand and foot. They seem to be a pair tied together in some gruesome three-legged race. Running wildly, they each try to match the other's uneven strides.

Obviously weaker than the woman, the man stumbles. He falls, face first, to the cold black earth, bringing the woman with him. She struggles to pull herself up to her knees. She is actually quite young, but her face is haggard and her eyes are hollow and dark-circled.

She frantically grabs the man's shirt collar. "Will!" she yells frantically into his tired, scraped face. "Do you hear me? We have to keep moving! They'll have noticed we're gone and have dogs after us by now. Will!" He groans and opens his eyes.

"Hurry, get up, it's only a little while to the river, I promise!" The desperation in her eyes borders on insanity. The man moans again and starts to pull his stocky frame up. "Tessie, my feet . . . they hurt." He reaches for his ill-shod left foot and howls in pain.

The thin girl rises shakily to her feet, bringing his muscular left arm up with her small right one. The skin around the iron shackles on her right wrist and ankle is badly swollen and red.

Tessie reaches down, grabs the man around the shoulders, and, with all of the strength in her tiny frame, pulls the man to a sitting position. Will tries to bring himself to stand up, but falters and falls back to the ground.

The young woman begins to cry. "Please, please get up. Do you know what they'll do if they find us, they'll . . . wait. What's that?"

Over the tallest treetops Tessie could see the tip of a yellow tower.

Dr. Allan Vorhees Lesley died in 1888. He and Mrs. Lesley, who had passed away in 1870, had no children. Although Dr. Lesley had several brothers, none of them could afford the upkeep of such a large estate. The house stood vacant for fifteen years.

Creeeaaak! The enormous wooden door of the dark mansion opened with Tessie's push. It had been left unlocked. Odd, she thought to herself.

Will stumbled along beside her. In the dark she could make out the massive Gothic arches and few pieces of furniture inside the seemingly deserted mansion. A metal statue of a Spanish conquistador glared at her from the banister at the foot of the stairs. Get out of here, he seemed to growl.

Immediately Will collapsed onto the hardwood floor of the parlor to the left of the foyer, grabbing a tasseled pillow from one of the dusty chairs. He fell asleep instantly.

Tessie reached down to rub the irritated skin around her shackled ankle. It was raw and crusted with blood.

It was then that she noticed that Will's ankle had turned a sickening shade of black-green and was oozing yellow pus from large blisters.

Gangrene. The terrible infection had eaten away at many a filthy inmate at the New Castle prison.

Repulsed by his sickening wounds, Tessie let out a silent sob and pulled as far away from the sleeping man as the iron chains would allow.

She gazed at her surroundings. Tessie hadn't noticed the rich decor of the mysterious mansion. Though covered with dust, she could make out the thick molding, the wood-paneled ceilings, the brightly colored walls, the few pieces of elegant Victorian furniture. A painting of a dark-haired woman over the marble fireplace seemed to stare directly at her. Tessie shivered and fell into a deep sleep.

In 1903, the Deemer family purchased the estate. When the new owners were going through the house, painting the thick molding and cleaning the Gothic bric-a-brac, they found a heap of something crouched in a corner.

It was a pile of human bones.

Mr. Deemer and the movers were frozen in place for a minute. No one said a word, the group staring at the forlorn skeletons.

Then one of the men bent down and started to gingerly brush the dust and dirt off the corpses. There were two of them, shackled together at the hand and foot with iron chains. Later studies showed that the bones belonged to a man and a woman.

Tessie awoke to the sound of birds chirping noisily outside. How long had she slept? Penetrating rays of sunlight were streaming through the black shutters of the cavernous bay window. It was late in the afternoon. They had to get moving.

Her stomach growled persistently. "Will!" she turned to the man and shook his shoulder. "Will! We have to get going. We're really close to the river. Let's just find some food and get out of here. Will?"

He hadn't moved an inch since she had started speaking to him. Tessie grasped his shoulder through his cotton shirt and shook him harder. "Will!" She touched his porous, beard-shadowed cheek. It felt rigid and clammy.

Tessie recoiled in terror. He couldn't be dead! What would she do? She grasped the wrist that had been attached to hers for so long and felt frantically for the pulse she would never find. She let out a twisted howl and tried to stand up, to get away from the dead man. His arm rose up with hers, but even when in a spasm she tried to run away from him, his two hundred pound body barely budged.

The tiny woman collapsed on the floor, sobbing, inadvertently kicking the corpse behind her as she tried to crawl her way to the front door. Somehow she managed to drag the body behind her to the wide archway leading to the main hall, where she again tried to right herself, panting profusely. Once to her feet, she grabbed the dead man's wrist with both hands and pulled him across the wooden floor towards the kitchen.

"I'll find a heavy kitchen knife and break through these chains. I have to! I have to!" she said to herself out loud, almost chanting the words, like a madwoman. "And then I'll run off on my own. They'll never find me. They won't take me back there!"

The kitchen was empty. The past occupants had apparently taken all of the utensils and kitchenware when they had deserted this scary old mansion.

Exhausted from dragging the corpse, Tessie fell against the wall, crying uncontrollably. She put her hands to her face to wipe away her tears. Attached to her right hand, the dead man's cold, bloated, black-blistered fingers brushed her cheek. Tessie stared at the sickening blue-green hand, then the empty face whose bloodshot eyes had fallen open in the commotion, staring up at her. A buzzing fly landed on the edge of Will's gaping mouth.

Tessie threw her head back and screamed.

The discovery of the two chained bodies in the house has raised many questions about the history of the mansion and its original owners. The current theory held by Mr. and Mrs. Class is that they were escaped convicts who happened onto the house by mistake, somehow let themselves in, and were too weak with disease to leave. They probably escaped from the nearby prison, where the ghastly conditions in those days led many prisoners to attempt escape. Unfortunately, like Will and Tessie in the story, many were not successful.

But is that the real answer behind the discovery of the bodies? The origin of the chained skeletons found in Lesley Manor may never be known.

§

"No."

His handsome face crumpled. "But . . . why?"

Emmaline sighed. "Because, Alfred. Because we've only known each other for three weeks and I'm leaving for Philadelphia tomorrow." She shifted her position in the high-backed chair. "Besides, you're always abroad, from what you've been telling me about flying to India and Sweden and Morocco . . . you couldn't ask me to be a wife to someone who's never there."

Turning away, Alfred cursed himself for his boasting that had backfired. He spun around again to see her sitting calmly in the chair beside her bed, an agonizingly passive expression on her heart-shaped face. She was absolutely beautiful, face half-clothed in light, but repellently cold.

Alfred, of course, was blinded by love of his frigid maiden. "I'd stop traveling if we were married, Emmaline.

I'd do whatever it takes to make you happy, you know that." He kneeled in front of her. "I love you, Emmaline. I think you love me too."

"You're wrong," she said simply, no hint of remorse on her face. "I'm sorry, Alfred. I'm not going to marry you."

Disgusted and embarrassed, he rose to his feet. Without a word, he walked out the door of the large room and slammed it behind him. Alfred went into his room in the manor and began to pack his things. There was no reason left for him to stay.

Millie Pataky's first encounter with the ghosts of Lesley Manor occurred shortly after her daughter Elaine purchased the house.

Millie had been an unbeliever in ghosts for seventy-five years. She had heard some of the folklore about the old house, but of course brushed it all off as being nonsense.

Only a few weeks after Elaine purchased Lesley Manor, Millie spent the night there, helping the Classes to settle into their new home. The house was not yet renovated and void of furniture.

That night, sleeping on a mattress on the mansion's floor, Elaine's mother had a strange dream.

She dreamt that she stood up and walked to the window of the room in which she slept. Standing outside the house was a broad-shouldered man in some type of a captain's uniform with a blue cape. He gazed up at her for a few seconds, and then bolted down the outside staircase and into the mansion's basement.

Alfred had packed as quickly as a scorned man could. He gathered his few belongings into a small suitcase and started down the second-floor hall to the stairs.

He passed the room Emmaline was staying in. Alfred stopped. He would never see her again. Perhaps she had changed her mind about his proposal. He wouldn't be able to live the rest of his life without knowing that he had at least bid her farewell.

Alfred cleared his throat quietly and put his suitcase down. The door was open just a crack. He heard what sounded like voices and muffled laughter inside. Alfred pushed on the door softly, swinging it open just in time to see his beloved Emmaline reach up and kiss the lips of a tall sandy-haired stranger.

A small, choked sound came from Alfred's throat. Blinding rage possessed him as he began to walk quickly toward them, and they sprang apart. Everything seemed to go in slow motion, from Emmaline's scream to the rhythmic motion of Alfred's steps. The last thing he saw was the surprise in the stranger's dark eyes as Alfred punched him hard in the jaw.

Emmaline screamed again, and it brought Alfred back to reality. He stared with shocked eyes at the man lying on the floor, blood dripping from his mouth. He looked at his hand. It hurt. Emmaline began to yell and cry, screaming things he couldn't understand. She backed away from him, terrified, and yelled for help.

Alfred turned away from her, still stunned by his violent actions, and began to run. He ran to the bending staircase, down the stairs, and through the giant hall, between the bewildered guests eating breakfast and the owners, yelling at him to stop from the front desk.

What had he done? He had felt the man's jaw crack under his powerful hand. Alfred had never hit another person before, and the thought of breaking a perfect stranger's jaw made his insides quiver.

And Emmaline. She had backed away from him as if he were a rabid wolf on the attack. She, who had been so tender and loving, who just a few days ago had sat with him on the white bench under the trees and talked of bird watching and safaris and flower gardening.

Alfred ran around to the back of the manor, into the meticulously manicured gardens. Where would he go? He had to escape quickly or he would be arrested.

His eyes fell on the basement steps. The owner of the mansion had bragged to him over dinner that the house was once part of the Underground Railroad, and that there was still a tunnel in the basement leading to the Delaware River. It could be his escape.

Alfred glanced once more to the window of Emmaline's room, silently cursing the selfish woman for the terrible grief she had brought upon him. Then, sensing someone coming around from the front of the house, he turned and ran down the basement steps, slipping on the slick stone of the second step and plummeting down to the hard cement floor.

A few weeks later, Millie stood in the front hall, holding the door open as movers were carrying large boxes of books and documents out of the house. As the last man was walking by her, an old book fell out of the box.

"You dropped this—" she started to say as she bent to pick up the book. Curious, Millie brushed off the dust from the cover. It was the journal of a pilot. Much later, Elaine Class discovered that many pilots had stayed in Lesley Manor around the turn of the century. Did the journal fall out by coincidence, or was it flung from the box?

§

The ghosts at Fox Lodge make life all the more interesting for those who live there. While Elaine's sister-in-law, Rose Pataky, was visiting from Ohio (on the same trip when Millie encountered the ghost of Jane Lesley), she had a rather unusual experience.

From the sitting room Elaine could watch her sister-in-law as she was walking down the bending grand staircase. Almost at the bottom of the stairs, Rose stopped abruptly. With a puzzled look on her face, she turned and went about halfway up the stairs, then stopped again. She continued to walk up and down the stairs increasingly slowly, her nose wrinkled and brow furrowed in concentration.

Elaine watched for several minutes in amusement before she finally asked Rose what was wrong. Her sister-in-law had been experiencing a strange, spicy smell on the staircase. The odd thing was, the odor was centered in only a few square feet of the staircase. Even though the smell was very strong, it was not dispersed throughout the room, as scents usually are when someone is wearing a fragrance. Before Rose could identify the strange smell, it disappeared.

When Rose arrived home in Ohio, she immediately called Elaine.

"I figured out what that smell was!" Rose exclaimed.

Elaine was prepared for the answer. "Cherry tobacco, right?"

"Right! Except it hasn't been lit yet."

Elaine had been experiencing the odd smells for quite a while in the house. Along with the smell of cherry tobacco, there was also a lighter, more female scent, an "old smell," as Elaine would describe it.

The scents were always centered in the amount of space a human being would occupy, in an area of no more than approximately nine square feet. The aroma would seem to drift around the room. On several occasions Elaine and her mother would "walk through the smell," giving them the feeling that they were walking through a person. These experiences parallel studies done by the famous psychic Sylvia Browne. She has stated that the strongest spirits have pungent odors, remnants of the character of the person.

No one is quite sure what the ghosts of Lesley Manor do when no one is around, but something definitely happens after sundown.

Before Fox Lodge, the bed and breakfast, was opened, the Class family did a good deal of redecorating and renovating on the mansion. Elaine and Lesa were forever painting, cleaning, and plastering the old house before it could be open for guests.

Oftentimes, after a long day of vacuuming the floors, washing the walls, and dusting the woodwork of a particular room, Lesa would give the room a once-over, making sure the room was completely clean and ready to be decorated. Something shiny would catch her eye.

On the floor in the middle of the room would be a shiny copper penny.

Lesley Manor was completed in 1855, at the height of the Victorian era. A well-known Victorian custom in America was the placing of a penny on top of the outside doorframe of every room in the house. This act was done to prevent evil spirits and ghosts from entering the room, a custom perhaps practiced by those living in Lesley Manor during Victorian times.

The finding of pennies in the middle of rooms that had been completely cleared out happened a few dozen times to Lesa. The first time it happened to Elaine, however, was after the first guests had stayed in Fox Lodge.

She had vacuumed the floors thoroughly, and after having taken the soiled linens and towels away, returned to the room to make sure it was in perfect order. Much to her surprise, there, lying in the middle of the floor in a very obvious place was a copper penny. The incident repeated itself quite a few times.

The pennies found by Lesa and Elaine seem to signify the ghosts' will to remain in their home, almost as if they are saying, "Here we are! Don't try to use pennies on us; we're one step ahead of you."

Lesa and Elaine spent a good deal of time cleaning the rooms of the mansion. They soon discovered that every day, immediately before sundown, strange voices would drift into the room. Gaping at each other with wide eyes, mother and daughter would listen to the echoes of loud conversations. The conversants were usually about six people: four men and two women. What they were talking about, Elaine and Lesa never found out. Paying heed to the ghosts' will, they always finished their work and left before sundown.

The voices they were hearing were not mumbled or fleeting; often whole sentences were distinguishable to mother and daughter as they renovated the house.

Once, the two were cleaning on opposite sides of a room when a loud, clear female voice broke the silence.

"It's looking really good in here. It really is."

The women whirled around and faced each other at the sound of the voice. They assured each other that neither of them had spoken, and they both had heard the same message.

Could it have been the voice of Jane Lesley, wanting to express her thanks at how enchanting her house had become? That is the belief held by Elaine and Lesa Class.

"It's looking really good in here." I must say, gazing up at the magnificent Gothic mansion, that I agree with the ghost.

A SCREAM ON THE SHORE

Cape Henlopen, Delaware

Electric lights were scarce but the Cape Henlopen beach that night was peculiarly bright. A clear full moon illuminated a wide strip of the otherwise black water in an uncanny white-blue. Two people, fishing rods in hand, walked along the strip of dark, damp sand near the ocean's edge where the water had been waist-level just hours before. They walked close enough to the surf so that every so often one valiant wave would just manage to reach out and touch their bare feet. The air was briny and crisp and fairly cool for the end of August. The pair talked quietly, or not at all, and enjoyed each other and the beauty of the night.

In the midst of the quiet, calm ambiance of the beach, a ragged scream pierced the air.

Marty and Michelle stopped walking. They joined hands and gave each other a frightened look, unconsciously backing up a little. They were not far from where they had left their car.

For a moment there was silence. Breathing heavily, Michelle zipped her jacket tighter to protect herself from the chill the wind had suddenly acquired. For about half a minute, the only sounds were the light wind and the soft breaking of the waves on the beach. They relaxed their grip on each other's hands and began to proceed.

Then there came a terrible shriek even louder than the previous one. Michelle looked up the beach and there she saw it -- what looked from far away to be a woman running madly toward them, huge mane of ghastly hair straggling behind her. From far away, her eyes seemed almost to glow. Her mouth was wide open in a frantically mad expression and she was ranting horrible guttural sounds of agony.

"Marty . . . Marty!" Michelle began to pull him down the beach away from the appalling specter that was approaching them fast, much too fast. Marty backed up with her, but as much as they wanted to get far away from the creature, neither of them was willing to turn away from her.

She ran directly at them, on a slight diagonal toward the water. In what seemed like no time the ghastly woman was within five feet of them. She didn't really stop running, but seemed to hop from one foot to another, pulling on her hair and dress as she looked out at the surf and then directly at Marty and Michelle, making Michelle quiver and gasp in terror and Marty stand frozen in place, grabbing onto his wife with both hands. Their mouths went dry; they couldn't speak a word.

Up close, they could see that she was missing most of her teeth. The woman's pupils and irises were so light that it appeared that her eyes were completely white unless one looked very closely. She was very pale and fairly old, with clammy skin and gnarled hair that looked like it had been pulled out in chunks. She only stood there for a few seconds, while no one said a word. Michelle and Marty began to quietly slink away…

SNAP! The thing turned her head as quickly as lightning from the pounding sea to the couple on the sand, producing a small scream from Michelle.

The terrible woman opened her toothless mouth and

let out a hoarse cry. When she talked it sounded as if her lungs were filled with sand. She spoke but one message, over and over again with increasing frenzy.

"Don't go...don't go in the water! DON'T GO IN THE WATER!!" She threw her head back to scream it again, then looked down, straight into Marty's eyes. "Don't go in," she whispered.

Scared to death, Marty and Michelle began to turn away. They had stumbled no more than a few feet when they heard one more agonizing shriek, this one longer and more terrible than ever before. Arms around the shuddering Michelle, Marty turned around to look with an almost irresistible attraction to the horrible sight, and gasped.

The woman was gone. There was not a sign of her anywhere on the beach.

Michelle pointed to the ground with a sharp intake of breath. Where the three of them had stood moments before, in the damp sand, were only two sets of footprints. Marty's and Michelle's.

Whatever the purpose of the hideous woman's message, she made her point. The couple left the beach the next day and did not return for more than three months. And it took nearly a year for either of them to go in the water.

Many legends of ghosts, witches, and pirate treasure surround Cape Henlopen, the site of the shipwreck of the infamous H.M.S. deBraak. The ship, which went down on May 25, 1798, has always been a maritime enigma. Legend has it that the ship's mysterious crew was a band of British pirates. It is said to be the enormous amount of foreign treasure in the hold that caused her to tip over in a fateful storm. Apparently, millions and millions of dollars in gold, silver, and jewels sank to the sea floor less than a mile from the shore of the Cape.

After nearly two centuries and tons of money spent on countless unsuccessful attempts to recover the legendary bounty, the disintegrated remains of the deBraak were finally raised on August 11, 1986. Though some artifacts were undoubtedly left on the muddy floor of the sea, many historically valuable relics were recovered. Gold coins, jewelry, buttons, shoes, and other objects found on the wreck, some of which are now on display in Delaware's Zwaanendael Museum, turned out to be worth about half a million dollars. As for the priceless treasure, it was never found.

Scholars are skeptical about the existence of such a treasure. But legend holds that a real fortune in plundered goods still lies at the bottom of the sea, unattainable to those seeking its wealth because of a vile sea witch who guards the sunken ship. If she does exist, she has been successful in guarding the loot for more than two hundred years, and her wrath may extend to anyone she thinks comes too close to the treasure.

THE RETURNING SPIRIT

Dover, Delaware

Deeply troubled, Arlene Stockwell was driving her daughter home from spending the night at another little girl's house. Everything had seemed okay when Arlene met her daughter's friend's parents; they had been polite, courteous, and pleasant.

But she couldn't shake the feeling that a deep, terrible sadness had been encircling the little girl's stepfather. For some reason, Arlene had been extra sensitive to what the man was feeling. The soft-featured, white-haired man of about 50 had seemed outwardly cheerful, but Arlene could sense a haze of despair about this man.

Her third-grade daughter seemed to have had an enjoyable stay at her friend's house, and Arlene did not want to upset her. She did not mention her disturbing thoughts, but the face of the man stayed with her as she pulled into the driveway of their Dover home.

That night, Arlene awoke in the wee hours of the morning. She was unsure of exactly what had jolted her from sleep, but something seemed to be beckoning her to come downstairs. She crept out of the room, careful not to wake her sleeping husband, and started to go down the steps.

Arlene could see into the living room from the

staircase, and the scene in that room was enough to stop her in her tracks.

The figure of a person was floating in the middle of the room. Its full body was not visible; the apparition was only from the shoulders up, much like a bust. Glowing radiantly, the figure was completely white. Curly white hair crowned its round, soft face, which was illuminated by a beautiful smile. "I thought at first that it was a woman, because it seemed to have soft, smooth features." Arlene knew that the ghost had somehow awakened her, and that it was aware of her presence, but "it *kind of* looked at me, but not directly at me. It almost looked *through* me."

Arlene was not afraid of the apparition. She felt that the ghost was completely peaceful. She groped for the light, and when she found it and switched it on, the figure vanished. The experience lasted only a moment. Arlene knew that the ghostly figure had not been merely a trick of the light, for her house was in a thickly wooded area and there was no outside light at all coming into the room. Filled with a calm peace left by the ghost, she went quietly to bed.

The next day, Arlene's daughter came home from school with dreadful news. Her friend had been called to leave school early that day, after her stepfather's body had been found in the woods very near Arlene's Dover home. He had left the house early that morning when his family was asleep and killed himself by firing a bullet into his head.

Arlene's mind flashed back to her late-night encounter with the ghost. A mental picture came into her head of the specter's beautiful smile, which at last she recognized. The ghost had been the spirit of this ill-fated man. Arlene was sure he must have known the sensitivity she had felt to his feelings, and he had come to her to let her know he was finally at peace.

Arlene never told her young daughter about her experience with the man's ghost. She never told the man's family, either, as they moved out of town sometime shortly after the tragedy.

THE HOUSE ON 6th STREET

New Castle, Delaware

Old New Castle can be considered the ghostly hangout of Delaware. Lesley Manor and the George Read II House, two of the most famous haunted houses in the state, boast New Castle addresses. But away from the shadow of the two mansions there is a more ordinary-looking house, where a closer look is required to find the paranormal. One need look no further than the third floor.

In a patch of sunlight on the carpeted floor sat the darling little boy, surrounded by his toys. Immersed in pushing the brightly colored cars and trucks in their circular track around his crouched body, the three-year-old at first did not notice the person who had joined him in the room. It wasn't until he heard the door slowly close that he looked up. "Mommy," he started to say, but she was not his mother.

Standing by the door was an old lady in a long gray

dress.

Her stern face and deep frown brought tears to the boy's eyes. He was too afraid to talk to her: she looked too mean. Who are you? he wanted to ask. He stared at the old lady and then back down to his toys. "Mommy..." he tried to whisper, his voice catching on his nervous tears.

The boy looked back up to see if the lady was still there. She was. Her black eyes held his. Her little lips were pinched in a straight line. Whimpering as he watched her, she slowly lifted her arm, pointing a bony, gnarled finger straight at him. The lips parted to form the rasping words, "Get out of here."

The three-year old boy did the only thing he could do: cry. He threw back his head, opened his mouth as wide as it would go and screamed. When he looked back to the doorway, the gnarled old specter was gone. Eric ran to the door and into the next room as fast as his little legs could carry him, sobbing, "Mama! Mama! Old lady scared me! Old lady scared me...Mama!"

His mother ran to meet him from the other room. "Sweetheart, what's wrong?" He buried his face in his mother's leg.

"The old lady scared me!"

"What old lady?"

"In there! She said, 'Get out'!"

As the son described to his mother in pouty gasps what the old lady looked like, the mother's curiosity and astonishment grew. Her son had seen a ghost, and she knew exactly whose ghost it was.

It wasn't until the sweet boy was sleeping peacefully in his bedroom on the second floor that his mother began to slowly climb the stairs to the third floor. She thought back on her ancestors and the history of the Old New Castle area. Her family had been among the first settlers of the beautiful locale along the Delaware River; they had lived in the close-knit New Castle society for a few hundred years.

She remembered that several years ago there had been a friend of her grandmother: a maiden aunt who would travel from house to house in the community, living with different nieces and nephews and their families. The house in which this old maid had taken her final breath was this very house on 6th Street, and she had been living on the third floor.

The atmosphere in the third floor room was calm and serene. The woman walked into the center of the room. When she spoke she knew that there was someone there to hear her.

"You know me. I'm your good friend's granddaughter. I remember how much she cared about you, as I do also."

She paused, and subconsciously began to stroke the quilt that was draped on the old rocking chair. "I know this is your home, and I don't want you to leave. But please do me a very important favor. Don't talk to my son. He's only a baby, and it frightens him. Thank you very much," she said in a soft voice. As she turned and walked quietly out of the room, she felt that she heard the faintest whisper of a promise, and could have sworn that she smelled a woman's sweet perfume mixed with the aroma of baking bread.

The old lady never scared the little boy again.

BABYSITTERS BEWARE

Wilmington, Delaware

"OK, Jason, time for bed."

"No, it's not."

"Yes it is, come on, let's go."

"No it's not. When do I have to go to bed?"

"Well, your mommy said at 8:30 and I've already let you stay up almost fifteen minutes extra—"

"But it's not bedtime, look at the clock!"

Susan smiled at the little boy and turned around to face the clock on the playroom wall by the doorway. She was surprised to see that the clock was set to 3:05. Its open face would have allowed Jason to change its black hands easily.

"See . . . I told you I didn't have to go to sleep." Jason looked up at her with innocent eyes. What a smart kid, to change the clock to push back his bedtime, Susan marveled. "Oh, no, you don't. Come here, silly." Susan reached over and grabbed the squirming boy in her arms. He giggled as she carried him into the kitchen. "My goodness, Jason, look at that! The kitchen clock says it's your bedtime."

When at last Jason was snuggled under the cozy covers in bed, Susan tread softly out the door and shut it quietly behind her. After peeking into baby Gretchen's bedroom to make sure she was sleeping soundly, Susan went downstairs quietly. Anticipating a quiet evening of watching television, she headed for the playroom: the room with the TV.

As Susan crossed the threshold into the playroom she stopped dead in her tracks. The door leading outside was wide open. She was absolutely sure it had been closed and locked when she had taken Jason upstairs; had he run back somehow and opened the door? She peeked out the doorway into the backyard. Everything seemed peaceful outside. All she could see were lightning bugs flying lazily through the muggy summer air. Puzzled, Susan pushed the door shut and locked and bolted it. With an uneasy feeling in her stomach, she proceeded to check all the other doors to make sure they were still closed and locked. They were. Jason must have just opened the playroom door when I wasn't looking, she told herself.

Susan walked back through the kitchen. A family who had lived in the Clares' house on Turnstone Drive in Brookmeade II had added an extra wing of the house off the kitchen to serve as a mother-in-law suite. The addition now served as a playroom for the Clare children.

Susan tuned the TV to an episode of "The Mary Tyler Moore Show" and reclined in the big rocking chair. She had been watching the program for about five minutes when she realized that her whole body had tensed, and that her hands were visibly shaking. Someone was watching her.

Susan looked around the room timidly. There was no one there. She couldn't pinpoint exactly what was wrong, but it was there: a heavy presence that watched her every move. The feeling that she for some reason should not be in that room made her blood run cold. Her eyes, the only part of her that was not afraid to move, darted nervously around the room.

And then something very cold slid slowly behind her neck. The icy gush whooshed behind her ear, rustling her hair ever so slightly. Susan gasped and held her breath as footsteps passed heavily by her chair. Feeling the form of a person behind her, she jumped and turned to see who was there. No one. An obvious new coldness was filling the room.

In a swift movement Susan sprang from the rocking chair. She bolted to the TV, turned it off, and ran from the room. Susan did not stop moving until she reached the family room, where she leaped onto the couch and grabbed a thick afghan. This is crazy, she told herself. If there is something dangerous in the house, it can get me just as easily in here as it could in the playroom! With not even a door between her and whatever was waiting in the other room, Susan waited for the Clares to return. Eyes wide, body tense, she sat in a corner of the couch and trembled with fear.

It was a beautiful summer day, several years from the time when Susan had baby-sat for Jason and Gretchen, that she ran into Mrs. Clare coming out of mass at St. Catherine's Church on Centerville Road. The two of them stopped and talked for a while about college and work and Jason and Gretchen.

About five minutes into the conversation, Mrs. Clare said, "Susan, there's a question I've always been dying to ask you. I never wanted to say anything when you were baby-sitting for us because I thought you might never come back!" Susan looked at her in astonishment as she continued, "When you were baby-sitting for us, did anything strange ever happen in our house?"

Susan had not thought of the weird happenings in the Clares' house in a long time. Mrs. Clare looked into her face intently as she replied, "What do you mean?"

"At the time you were baby-sitting for us, we were living with a ghost."

"A ghost!" The word had never come to Susan's mind when she was baby-sitting.

"Yes. I know it sounds strange, but only one part of the house was really haunted: the playroom." Susan stood shocked on the church steps as Mrs. Clare continued, "The ghost never harmed us or the children in any way, but she did scare us sometimes! Strange things would happen in that room. We would feel freezing cold breezes, the presence of someone else, the feeling that someone was watching you. Sometimes she would even change the hands on the clock."

Change the clock. Susan gasped. "I thought Jason was doing that because he didn't want to go to bed!" Jason was an extra-intelligent child but she had been giving him too much credit!

"No, that was her. We think she kept changing the clocks to read the time that she died. Now, I never saw her, but Mr. Clare did. He saw an old woman once, at the top of the stairs . . ."

John was walking toward the steps when he glanced up and saw the old woman. There was a faint ethereal glow about the figure that startled Mr. Clare, and he gasped. She had a feeling about her as if she were from another time. In the split second that she was there at the top of the stairs, John could sense that she was very dead. She looked neither at him nor at anything else in the room, and then she was gone. For a minute he wondered if he had imagined the spectral woman, but he knew he had not. He could still feel her in the room.

"One night I was home alone with the kids. Mr. Clare was on a business trip. We were awakened in the middle of the night by the most horrible sound: a terrible clanging that shook the entire house. It sounded like there was an air raid or something. I ran to the kids' rooms, terrified. I didn't know what was making the noise, but it sounded like the whole house was going to explode. Then as quickly as it started, the noise stopped. We figured out where it was coming from and the only explanation was that the ghost must have been banging on the pipes in the basement. Judging from the fury that she did it with, we thought she must have been very angry about something. That is when we had a priest come and bless the house. It wasn't an exorcism; he simply came into the house and prayed and sprinkled holy water in every room and every closet. He came only once, and we never heard from the old ghost again."

It wasn't too long after the ghost left them that the Clares gained some insight about who she was and why she had been haunting them. Mr. Clare was outside in the yard when his next-door neighbor appeared on the other side of the fence.

Eventually, John Clare led the conversation to the subject of the old woman who used to live in the in-law suite. The people next door had lived there when she lived in the Clares' house. Curious, John Clare began to ask his neighbor a few questions about the woman, when she had died and such.

The mother-in-law had moved in with the young couple because the wife was expecting a baby. The two of them wanted her to stay with their new child, her grandchild, and help them take care of him. "She was so tickled with the idea of becoming a grandmother and taking care of that baby. Such a sad thing, though. She died before she could meet any of her grandchildren. She never got to take care of the little ones."

The old woman who haunted the playroom of the Clares' house was most likely this woman, looking for the grandchildren she never met. Perhaps she merely wanted to inspect the young baby-sitter who was taking her place.

SHANNON'S RING

Wilmington, Delaware

Shannon stared into the black barrel. Not quite sure how she had managed to sneak it out of her father's possession, she marveled at its unexpected heaviness.

Her hands were cold. Had it all come to this?

Shannon's hopeless crusade had ended here, leaving her gazing at the heavy black object in her hand. She had tried so hard to find the one thing that could have been her savior, but they had taken that, as they had taken all that could make her happy ever again.

Hers would go unnoticed. In the middle of the Great Depression, suicide happened all the time.

Nikki tossed and wiggled under the covers. She didn't usually have this much trouble falling asleep. For nearly an hour she had drifted in and out of light slumber, caught in the groggy, dreamlike stage between being asleep and awake.

She turned onto her back. The lump of blankets next to her gave a little snore and a soft sigh. Anthony always slept like a log.

Her eyes finally opened and she gave up the struggle. Maybe I'm not used to sleeping in a different house, she thought. But she had slept perfectly soundly the previous three nights she and her husband had spent in the Wilmington row house that they had just bought.

Amid the large brown boxes strewn about, the bedroom was beginning to take shape. Nikki liked the way they had arranged the furniture and decorated the walls. Her eyes surveyed the room, landing on the wicker-framed mirror on the opposite wall.

She had never noticed it before, but the mirror and her bed were at such an angle that from her position she could see clearly the reflection of the closed closet door. Not sure why this new discovery so held her attention, she watched intently as the heavy door's crystal doorknob began to turn.

Nikki sank back into the pillow. I must be dreaming, she thought to herself. But she knew she was not asleep when she heard the slight creak as the door began to open, ever so slowly.

Horrified but unable to do anything but stare, Nikki watched the reflection in the mirror. A small white hand had appeared gripping the doorknob. It was quickly joined to a thin bare arm, a soft pink nightgown, a head of dark curls. A dark-haired young woman was opening the closet door.

The girl moved quickly. Nikki trembled and watched her open the door and go into the closet. She rummaged through the closet from top to bottom, obviously searching for something.

She soon emerged from inside the door, and Nikki could finally see her face. She glowed with old-fashioned natural beauty. Fascinated, Nikki stared at the girl's lace-edged nightgown and shiny brown Botticelli-esque curls. Suddenly she looked up with deep brown eyes filled with tears and seemed to notice Nikki in the bed.

Nikki gasped and held her breath. The girl's eyes were pools of sadness and they held Nikki's. Her expression was one of the deepest torments, contorted in pain as she tried to speak to Nikki. Her lips moved frantically, not uttering a single sound. The reflection seemed to grow closer and closer, and Nikki recoiled in horror as the girl suddenly vanished. The closet door stood open.

He had been standing in the park by an old tree the first time she had seen him. The image of his sharp expression and confident, easy stance was still with her. The tree had become their mailbox, their secret meeting place. Sometimes she would catch him as he was leaving her a letter. As she turned the corner, she'd see his tall form standing by the old oak, and then he'd smile and to her the sun would shine a little brighter.

And sometimes there would only be a letter, and it would join the others in the bundle under her mattress. In her blissful foolishness she never really thought that they would find them.

"Are you sure it wasn't just a dream?" It was Anthony's first reaction to the story she told him in the morning.

Nikki stared into her coffee cup. She wasn't sure what she had seen. Maybe she had only imagined the dark-haired girl.

But then two nights later it happened again. The same girl in the mirror, going into the closet and then coming out, staring at Nikki and desperately trying to say something to her. This time Nikki lunged in terror at the sleeping Anthony, wrapping her arms around him and burrowing her face into his back.

"She's here again! Look, look!"

Anthony sat up in the bed. "There's no one there."

Nikki turned quickly. The girl was gone, but the door to the closet was wide open. "Well, look. I closed the closet door before I went to bed, and now it's open."

Frustrated because Anthony didn't believe her story but exhausted from fright, Nikki laid her head on his shoulder and tried to fall asleep.

They could never understand. They didn't even want to meet him; they were too preoccupied with their old-fashioned bias to see what was right.

But no amount of pleading sobs would ever budge her parents. Her father's thunderous phrase still reverberated in her head.

"I'll never let my daughter marry a Jew."

The words were final.

Almost a week had passed, and Nikki had spent many sleepless nights laying awake waiting for the spectral girl, but she hadn't come. Sleep was infrequent and full of dreams of young women weeping from grief. Nikki had finally fallen asleep one night when she was roused by a hand on her shoulder. Her eyes popped open.

"Nikki, what's wrong?" Anthony was leaning over her with a concerned look on his face.

"Nothing, why?" She yawned and blinked.

"Were you crying?"

"No, why?"

"I could have sworn I heard you crying."

Nikki propped herself up onto her elbows, excited. "Maybe it was the…"

"Shhh!" Anthony's eyes were as big as saucers and he was staring past her. She turned around to the sound of something wiggling the doorknob to the closet.

Nikki backed up into Anthony, who clutched her hand as the knob turned and the door creaked wide open, slamming into the wall behind it. The closet's open mouth gaped at them. And the reflection of a ghastly black-eyed girl was standing in the mirror, her mouth open in a silent scream.

It's gone, it's gone, it's gone. Shannon had torn apart the house looking for the one thing that had caused her so many tears but that she couldn't live without. Where could they possibly have hidden it? How could they possibly have taken it?

The fact that they had managed to steal the one last token of his love seemed to confirm the fact that they could control her life. She had to have it back, and with it would come the hope she was quickly losing. She'd find a way to be with him, somehow.

But with every moment she searched she saw more and more that they would win.

While at work the next day, Nikki contacted her realtor. She was convinced that their house was haunted, and she was not looking forward to spending another night there.

The realtor claimed to know nothing of ghosts in the house, and Nikki believed her. She said that the people from whom Anthony and Nikki had bought the house, Daniel and Irene Murphy, were a nice pair of first-generation Irish Americans. They were the original owners of the house, and had lived in it for more than fifty years. Nikki and Anthony had never met them. "They're good people," the realtor commented.

"Did they have any daughters?" Nikki asked. With long dark hair, she wanted to add.

"Not that I know of. They only have one son, Danny, who lives in upstate New York."

The realtor couldn't give her any more information. Nikki hung up unsatisfied. Who was the dark-haired girl?

For the next few nights, Nikki and Anthony slept in one of the other two bedrooms. Disappointed that the house she once had loved now held something that terrified her, Nikki was not sure what to do.

That Saturday dawned brilliant and beautiful. Nikki decided to tend to the small garden in the backyard. Every tiny sound in the house was making her jump with fright, and she needed some fresh air to calm her nerves.

In the yard next door, Linda Prior was watering her lawn. As Nikki planted her petunias, she struck up a conversation with the amiable woman, who asked how things were in the new house.

"Oh, great," Nikki responded, hoping Linda wouldn't notice the trace of hesitation in her voice. She didn't.

"It's such a nice neighborhood," Linda said. "And such a pretty home. The Murphys stayed here as long as they could. They just didn't want to leave."

Nikki got a slight chill at the mention of the previous owners. It reminded her of the ghost. "I've never had the pleasure of meeting them myself, but I've heard that they're nice people."

"Oh yes, Dan and Irene were always extremely kind, generous people. Very quiet, though. Mostly they kept to themselves," she paused. "Though I've heard they were a lot less withdrawn before their daughter died."

Nikki tried not to show her astonishment. The girl! "Their daughter?"

Linda continued, apparently pleased to be the informant. "When my husband and I moved in, their son, Danny, had just graduated from college. We always just assumed that he was their only child. We found out later from another neighbor that Danny had an older sister, Shannon. I think she was about twenty when she died. Awful."

"How did she die?"

"I never found out. No one really knew, and they said that even her obituary was ambiguous. By the way the Murphys would never even mention her name, I think that she came to some terrible end. And I always thought that the reason Dan and Irene lived there for so long was because of an almost guilty feeling that they could never leave the house where Shannon died."

ꙮ

All of the furniture in the house had been arranged and all of the boxes unpacked, except in one room. "We can't be afraid to go in the bedroom *forever*," Anthony declared.

"Of course. We can finish that room today," Nikki replied. He was talking about Shannon's room. The thought chilled her.

Lit in the yellow lamplight, the room did not look nearly as morbid as Nikki had been imagining it for days. When the bed and dressers and nightstand were satisfactorily in place, the few knickknacks were arranged and the lamps and clock were positioned, Anthony went without hesitation to the door of the closet, a stack of brown packing crates in his arms.

"You know," he said with his head in the closet, "it's not so bad in here. No zombies."

"None at all?" Nikki smiled and stepped hesitantly toward the door.

"Well, just a few. They're not so bad."

She laughed, and joined him in the doorway. "This molding around the frame is nice," she said. "It's a shame that it faces the inside of the closet."

"Strange," he agreed. "It needs a new coat of paint." Anthony ran his hand along the frame on the inside of the door. Abruptly he stopped. "Hey, what's this?"

A tiny corner of paper was sticking out from between the frame and the wall. At first they thought it was just a scrap piece of paper, but when Anthony tried to pull it out, it wouldn't budge. After much tugging and working at the little piece of yellowed paper, Anthony pulled out a small square, folded many times and taped shut. A lump in the middle of it suggested that it contained something.

Nikki and Anthony looked at each other in astonishment. "I wonder what it is!" she whispered with excitement.

Nikki peeled open the tape with the distinct feeling that they had stumbled onto a very special relic, an important piece of someone's life. The yellowed paper had been folded and unfolded many times. Being careful not to tear it, Nikki opened the little package. Something shiny fell out and hit the floor.

"What a beautiful ring!" Nikki exclaimed as she bent to pick it up. She held the little golden circle up to the light. It was a simple gold band with one diamond, a small one, but it sparkled with fiery life.

Nikki was admiring the ring when Anthony whispered, "It's a letter." He was staring down at the paper in his hand. Clutching the diamond ring in her hand, Nikki began to read.

My Dear Shannon,

I love you from the bottom of my heart. That will never change for the rest of my days. I wish your parents approved of me, but I know now neither of us will ever be able to change their minds. That is why I am writing to tell you I am leaving on Saturday to work for my uncle in Philadelphia. I'll have a room over his store and he will pay me fifteen dollars a week.

I will never see you again, Shannon. This is the last letter I will leave you. And even though you will never be able to let anyone see you wearing this ring, I want you to have it. Hide it in a safe place and keep me always in your heart, as I will keep you in mine.

Love Always,

Marvin

A heart-shaped jewelry box on a shelf in her bedroom now holds Shannon's ring. With the discovery of the letter from Marvin, it appeared Shannon's spirit could finally rest. Her ghost was never seen again.

The italicized parts of this story are how the author imagines Shannon's story may have happened. Perhaps Shannon's spirit had been waiting for the chains of bigotry to fall, and for a time when the world could accept the love she and a boy named Marvin had once shared.

◈ Bibliography ◈

Adams, Charles, and Seibold, David. Shipwrecks, Sea Stories, and Legends of the Delaware Coast. Reading: Exeter House, 1989.

Anderson, Jean. "The Most Haunted House." The Haunting of America. Boston: Houghton Mifflin, 1973.

Haas, Cliff. "Ghosts Haunt Gov.: Or Maybe It's Just Another Democrat." State News 19 April 1978.

Hart, Emily. Woodburn: The Governor's House of Delaware. (Report)

Jefferson, John. "Legends About Ghosts, Slaves Surround Historic Woodburn." Southern Delaware Magazine May 1996.

Townsend, George Alfred. The Entailed Hat, or Patty Cannon's Times. New York: Harper & Bros., 1883.

◈ About the Author ◈

At the first printing Caroline Woods is a sixteen-year-old junior at Alexis I. du Pont High School in Greenville, Delaware. She enjoys playing lacrosse and field hockey, swimming, acting, reading, and being the junior class president and a pom in the marching band.

This is Caroline's first book. She plans to major in English in college and write many more.

If you've heard something go bump in the night and want to share your Delaware ghost story, please contact Caroline Woods at:

Carocour@aol.com

Thank you and sleep tight...